Dragon Danger

Cynthia Rider • Alex Brychta

OXFORD

UNIVERSITY PRESS

Floppy was dreaming about
dragons.

Floppy saw a baby dragon with its mother.

The mother dragon saw Floppy.

"Go away," she roared.

The dragon roared again and
flapped her wings.

She flew towards Floppy.

"Oh help!" he said.

WHOOSH! Flames came out
of the dragon's mouth.

Floppy hid, but the
dragon saw him.

Floppy ran onto a bridge.
WHOOSH! More flames
came out of the dragon's mouth.

"Help!" said Floppy.
"The bridge is on fire."

Floppy ran back across the
bridge.

He ran past a rock and saw the
baby dragon again.

The mother dragon roared at
Floppy. She flew up onto a
high rock.

Oh no! The rock started to fall.

CRASH! The rock fell
down . . .

but Floppy pulled the baby
dragon out of danger.
"Phew! Just in time," he said.

What a brave dog!

Why did the
mother dragon
roar at Floppy?

Why couldn't
Floppy hide from
the dragon?

How do you think
Floppy felt when the
rock started to fall?

What other
dragon stories
do you know?

A Maze

Help Floppy find his way out of the dragon's maze.

Useful common words repeated in this story and other books in the series.

again   but   came   of   onto   out   said   saw   she   the

Names in this story: Floppy